This yearbook belongs to:

. . . .

ISBN 978-1-338-14924-1

10 9 8 7 6 5 4 3 2 1   17 18 19 20 21

Printed in China   38
This edition first printed 2017

Scholastic Inc., 557 Broadway, New York, NY 10012

Harry Potter™

GRYFFIN... RAVENCLAW

SLYTHERIN

HUFFLEPUFF

HUFFLE PUFF

SLYTHERINI

PRACO

DORMIENS NUNQUAM

TITILLANDUS

HOGWARTS

A CINEMATIC YEARBOOK: IMAGINE, DRAW, CREATE

SCHOLASTIC

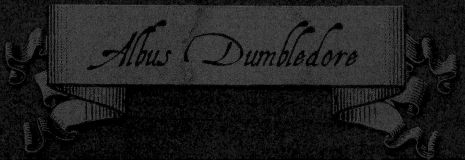

Albus Dumbledore

CONTENTS

A Wizarding Welcome! 10

My Magical Family 11

Diagon Alley 12

Journey to Hogwarts 14

My First Year at Hogwarts

Fold-Out Diary 16

The Great Hall 17

The Sorting Hat 18

Hogwarts Houses Postcards 19

Special Subjects 22

Hogwarts Timetable 23

Potions Class 24

Harry Potter Poster 25

Wonderful Wands 28

Special Delivery! 30

The Marauder's Map 32

Amazing Animagi 34

Quidditch Trials 36

Quidditch Postcards 37

Breaking News 40

Magical Creatures 42

Charm School 44

Helpful House-Elves 46

Turning Time 48

Hermione Granger Poster 49

Mirror, Mirror 52

Beastly Book 53

King Aragog 54

Ron Weasley Poster 55

The Triwizard Tournament 58

Magical Memories 60

A WIZARDING WELCOME!

Welcome to your Hogwarts Yearbook! Discover what it would be like to spend your first year at Hogwarts School of Witchcraft and Wizardry.

Harry Potter is stunned when he receives his letter, signed by Professor McGonagall.

Hundreds of acceptance letters fill number four Privet Drive.

My MAGICAL *Family*

Harry had a Muggle-born mother and a pure-blood father, making him a half-blood.

James Potter
FATHER
(pure-blood)

Lily Potter
MOTHER
(Muggle-born)

Harry Potter
SON
(half-blood)

KEY

PURE-BLOOD – a person whose family only has magical heritage.

HALF-BLOOD – a person who has both magical and Muggle heritage.

MUGGLE-BORN – a witch or wizard born of non-magical parents.

MUGGLE – a non-magical person.

SQUIB – a wizard-born, non-magical person.

What is unique about your family? Create your own family tree here.

DIAGON ALLEY

Hagrid brings Harry to Diagon Alley to buy all the required school supplies for his first year at Hogwarts.

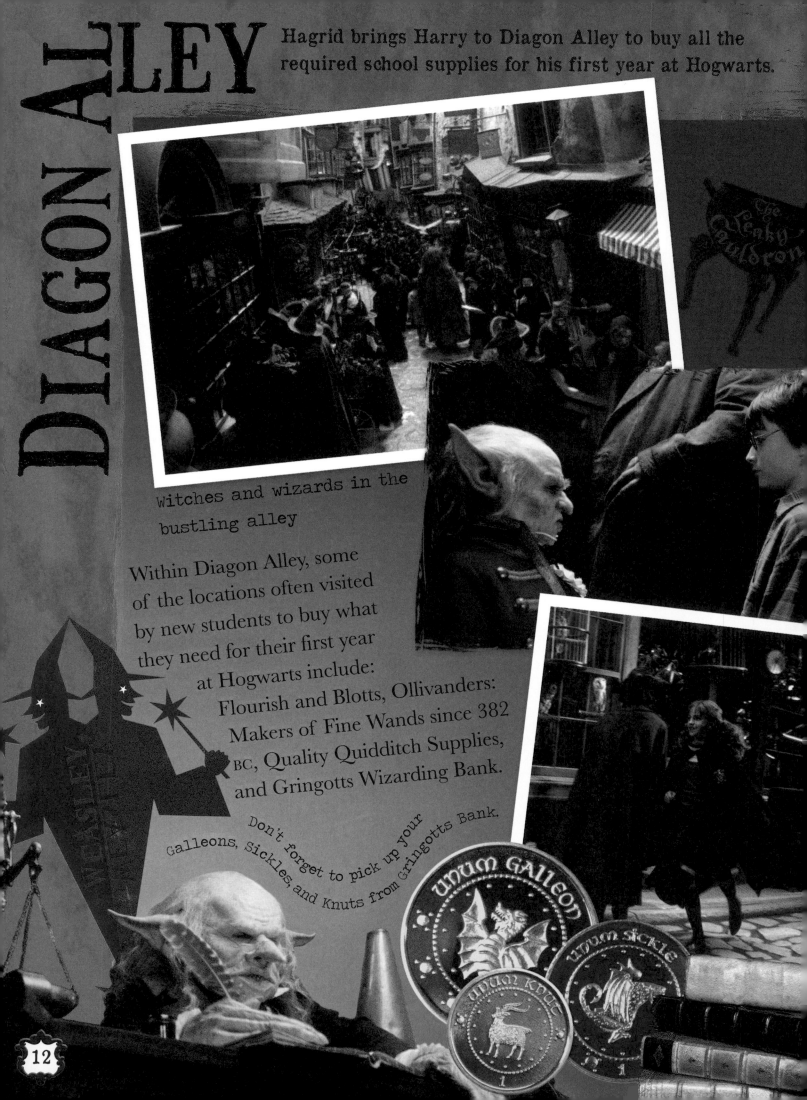

Witches and wizards in the bustling alley

Within Diagon Alley, some of the locations often visited by new students to buy what they need for their first year at Hogwarts include: Flourish and Blotts, Ollivanders: Makers of Fine Wands since 382 BC, Quality Quidditch Supplies, and Gringotts Wizarding Bank.

Don't forget to pick up your Galleons, Sickles, and Knuts from Gringotts Bank.

The Leaky Cauldron

UNUM GALLEON

UNUM SICKLE

UNUM KNUT

Use this page to sketch what you would
buy if you were to visit Diagon Alley:

Flourish and Blotts

Ollivanders

**Quality Quidditch
Supplies**

Gringotts

JOURNEY TO HOGWARTS

All aboard! The Hogwarts Express departs from Platform Nine and Three-Quarters at King's Cross station, London, and travels to the village of Hogsmeade.

9¾ HOGWARTS EXPRESS

Originally built by Muggles as a steam locomotive, this impressive engine now runs on magic.

No. 257 for ONE-WAY Ticket to be shown upon demand
LONDON to HOGWARTS
Platform 9¾

Ron shows Harry how to enter the secret platform through a solid brick wall.

HOGWARTS EXPRESS 5972

Record your first-year memories in your very
own Hogwarts diary. Use the fold-out pages
to imagine what it would be like to experience
Hogwarts for yourself.

Your HOGWARTS *Diary*

Think about what you
would pack in your trunk.
Would you want your
friends to ride on the
Hogwarts Express with you?

If you're not sure what to write,
read on through the yearbook and
return to some of the pages later.

What would be your perfect way to find out about your acceptance into Hogwarts?

Write about it or draw it here.

Letter *of* Acceptance

Head of HOUSE

Who would be your dream Head of House?

Fill in the teacher's profile below, and then draw a picture of how this person would look.

Full name:

House:

Appearance:

Subject(s) taught:

The GREAT Hall

THE ★★★★★★★★ SORTING ★★★ HAT

The ancient Sorting Hat decides which of the four houses Hogwarts students are placed into. The houses are Gryffindor, Hufflepuff, Ravenclaw, and Slytherin.

Slytherin! The Sorting Hat decides instantly when placed upon the head of Draco Malfoy.

RAVENCLAW

GRYFFINDOR

HUFFLEPUFF

SLYTHERIN

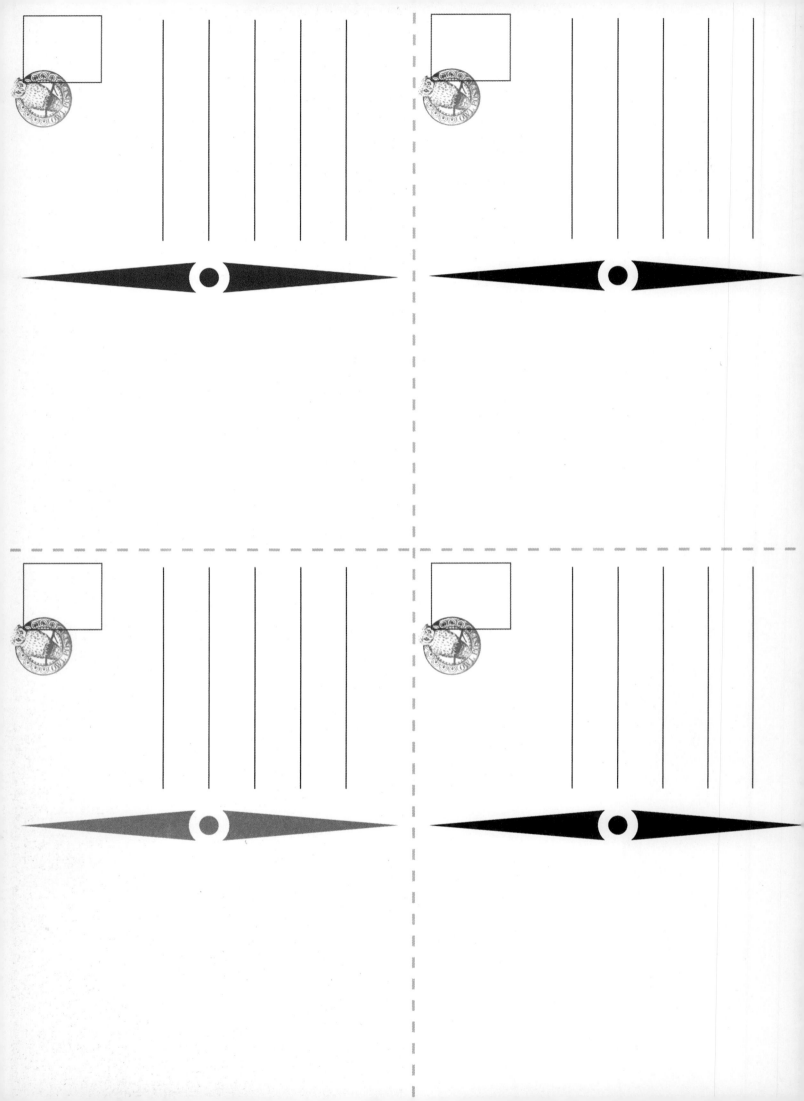

Which house could you imagine yourself part of?
Read the descriptions and circle your choice.

GRYFFINDOR
If you are brave, loyal, and protective of your friends, the Sorting Hat may put you in this lionhearted house. Gryffindors are not afraid to be honest and tell the truth, even if it's not always welcomed.

HUFFLEPUFF
Hardworking Hufflepuffs are dedicated and patient. They value fair play ahead of wanting to be the best.

RAVENCLAW
Ravenclaws are clever and wise. They are often gifted students who excel when it comes to taking exams.

SLYTHERIN
Slytherins are extremely ambitious, cunning, and resourceful, and work hard to get what they want.

SPECIAL

SUBJECTS

When Harry, Ron, and Hermione attended their first year at Hogwarts, they had to take seven subjects: Defense Against the Dark Arts, Transfiguration, Charms, Potions, History of Magic, Astronomy, and Herbology. Flying lessons (on broomsticks) were also required.

If you could attend one of these classses, which would it be? Write about what you would learn here:

_____

_____

_____

_____

_____

_____

_____

_____

_____

HOGWARTS
Timetable

Complete your timetable with
two lessons for each subject.
Add in four flying lessons.

Then decide what you could
do with your free periods.

	Lesson 1	Lesson 2	Lesson 3	Lesson 4
Monday			L	
Tuesday			U	
Wednesday			N	
Thursday			C	
Friday			H	

POTIONS Class

In Potions class, Hogwarts students learn how to brew potions correctly.

Hermione once brewed Polyjuice Potion to transform Ron and Harry into Crabbe and Goyle!

LIBATIUS BORAGE's
ADVANCED POTION-MAKING

Bezoars

If you could create a potent potion of
your own, what ingredients would you use
and what would the potion do?

WONDERFUL
Wands

Lord Voldemort's yew wand
spells trouble at the
Ministry of Magic.

Wands are magical objects that
choose their owners. These long,
thin rods of wood have a magical
substance embedded into their core.

Harry's wand is made from holly
with a phoenix feather core.

Check one box from each column to choose your perfect wand.

Wood	Magical core	Length	Flexibility
English oak ☐	phoenix feather ☐	10" ☐	supple ☐
holly ☐	Thestral tail hair ☐	12" ☐	springy ☐
vine ☐	dragon heartstring ☐	14" ☐	bendy ☐
yew ☐	unicorn tail hair ☐	other length ☐	inflexible ☐
hawthorn ☐	troll whisker ☐		
red oak ☐			
alder ☐			

Now draw your ideal wand!

SPECIAL DELIVERY!

When Harry and Ron missed the Hogwarts Express at the start of their second year, they flew to school in the Weasley family's flying car. Mrs. Weasley later sent Ron a deafening Howler to let him know just how angry she was!

"RONALD! WEASLEY! HOW DARE YOU STEAL THAT CAR! I AM ABSO DISGU YOUR NOW F INQUI AND IT'S ENTIR YOUR FAULT! IF YOU PUT ANOTHER TOE OUT OF LINE WE'LL BRING YO TRAIGH and Ginny gratu on makin our father So

CAUTION
Once a Howler has been read, it will burst into flames!

Ron wasn't happy to receive a Howler from his furious mother.

Think about a time when you've done something silly. Write a Howler from a parent, grandparent, or teacher, or send a Howler to someone you know.

THE MARAUDER'S MAP

The Marauder's Map shows the location of everyone at Hogwarts.

Messrs.
MOONY, WORMTAIL, PADFOOT & PRONGS
are proud to present

HOGWARTS

The
MARAUDER'S MAP

Can you draw a map of how you think Hogwarts would be laid out?
Place an X where you would most like to be.

AMAZING Animagi

Animagi are witches or wizards who can morph themselves into animals. Animagi are closely linked to personality. Sirius Black's Animagus is a black dog named Padfoot.

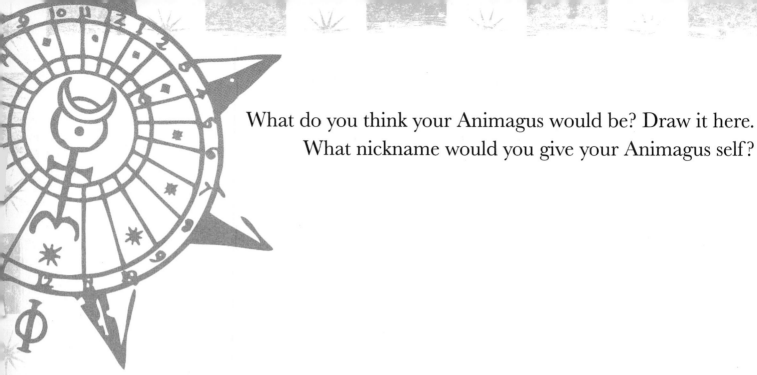

What do you think your Animagus would be? Draw it here.
What nickname would you give your Animagus self?

My Animagus is called:

Quidditch
TRIALS

Quidditch is a magical game on broomsticks that has been played in the wizarding world for centuries. It is Harry's favorite sport.

Harry lines up alongside Gryffindor captain, Oliver Wood.

RACING BROO

YOU CAN SCORE GRYFFINDOR!

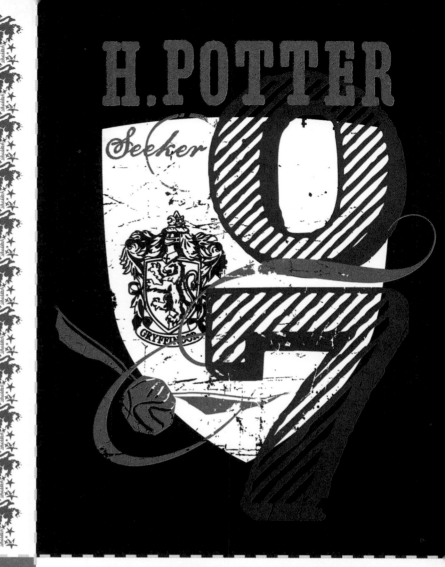

H. POTTER
Seeker
GRYFFINDOR

R. WEASLEY
02
Keeper
GRYFFINDOR

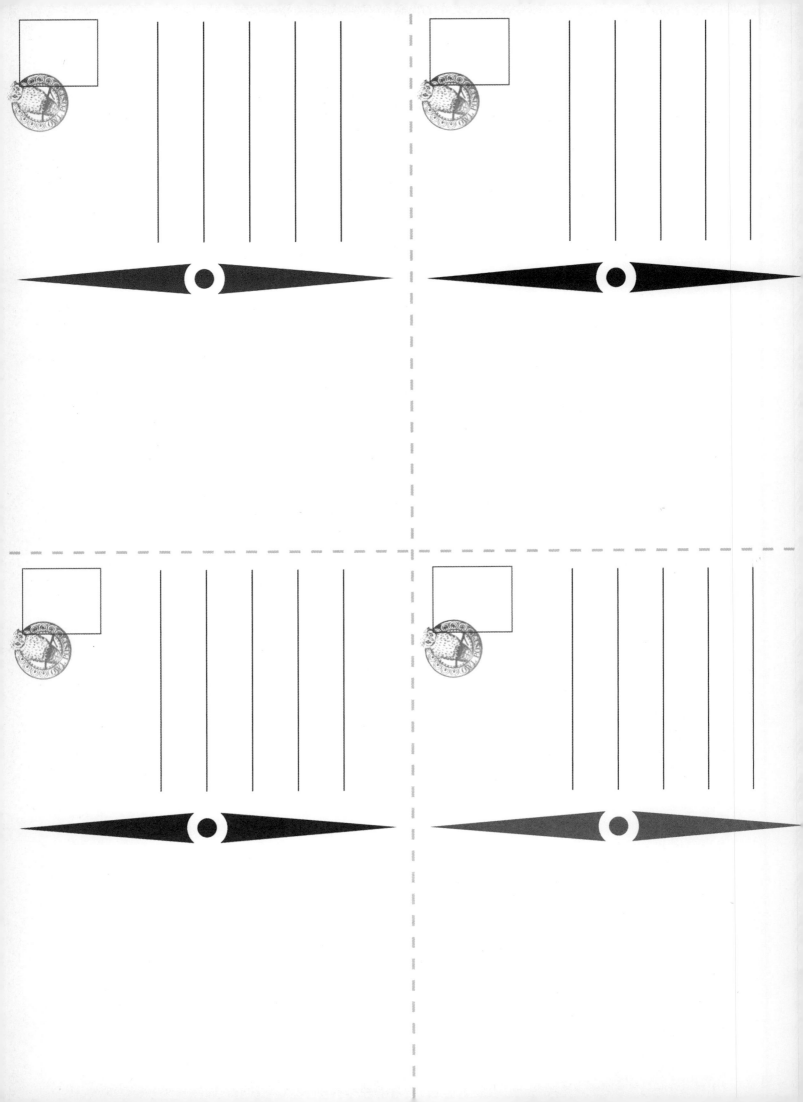

Imagine you were on a Quidditch team.
What would your Quidditch robes and broom look like?
What position would you want to play?

I would be a:

Keeper☐   Chaser☐   Beater☐   Seeker☐

BREAKING NEWS

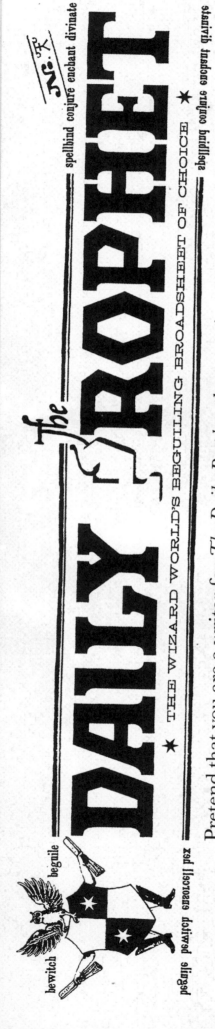

The DAILY PROPHET

★ THE WIZARD WORLD'S BEGUILING BROADSHEET OF CHOICE ★

spellbind conjure enchant divinate

charm hocus-pocus sorcery bewitch

beguile

bewitch

bewitch conjure enchant divinate

bedazzle

bedazzle hex

Pretend that you are a writer for *The Daily Prophet*, the top wizarding newspaper. Grab your quill and write a story that is worthy of being front-page news.

41

MAGICAL CREATURES

Hogwarts students can choose to take Care of Magical Creatures in their third year. Would you choose to learn about Hippogriffs, Thestrals, and unicorns?

The Forbidden Forest is home to a cluster of Acromantulas.

Luna reaches out to stroke a skeletal Thestral.

Buckbeak is a Hippogriff, a creature that has the head of an eagle and the body of a horse.

Create your own magical creature, then write its name below.

My magical creature is called:

Charm School

The Patronus Charm is a difficult piece of magic that offers protection against Dementors. Harry's Patronus is a stag.

EXPECTO PATRONUM!

Harry casts his stag Patronus when faced with hundreds of Dementors at the Great Lake.

During Harry's fifth year at Hogwarts, he taught the Patronus Charm to his classmates when they formed Dumbledore's Army.

Imagine you were able to conjure your own Patronus. What kind of animal do you think it would be?

HELPFUL HOUSE-ELVES

House-elves are magical creatures that loyally serve their wizarding family. Dobby once worked for the Malfoys, while Kreacher served Sirius Black's family.

Dobby visited the Dursley house to warn Harry not to return to Hogwarts.

Cranky Kreacher faithfully served Sirius and his family.

Dobby fought bravely at Malfoy Manor during the second wizarding war.

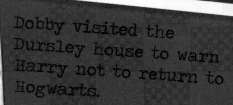

KREACHER HAS BEEN... WATCHING.
KREACHER ALWAYS WATCHES.

A house-elf is granted freedom when they are given clothing by their master. If you could, what kind of clothes would you give a house-elf to set him or her free?

Harry Potter NOT back Hogwarts School of Witchcraft and Wizardry this year!

Hermione turns the magical Time-Turner three times to travel a few hours into the past.

Hermione and Harry once used a magical time-traveling device called a Time-Turner to rescue Sirius Black and Buckbeak the Hippogriff.

TURNING TIME

Imagine you had a Time-Turner of your own.
What would you use it for?

Mirror Mirror

Stare into the Mirror of Erised and the deepest desire of your heart will be revealed.

Imagine you had a chance to look into the Mirror of Erised. What do you think the Mirror would show you? Draw it below.

BEASTLY BOOK

The Monster Book of Monsters is required reading for all students in Hagrid's Care of Magical Creatures class. The book will attack anyone who attempts to open it, so handle with care!

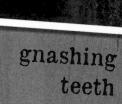

Draw lines to label the parts of this vicious volume.

gnashing teeth

all-seeing eyes

matted fur

hissing tongue

spiky tentacles

KING ARAGOG

Aragog the Acromantula lived in the Forbidden Forest. Hagrid hatched him from an egg, but he soon grew to an enormous size.

Aragog, king of arachnids, with his owner, Hagrid

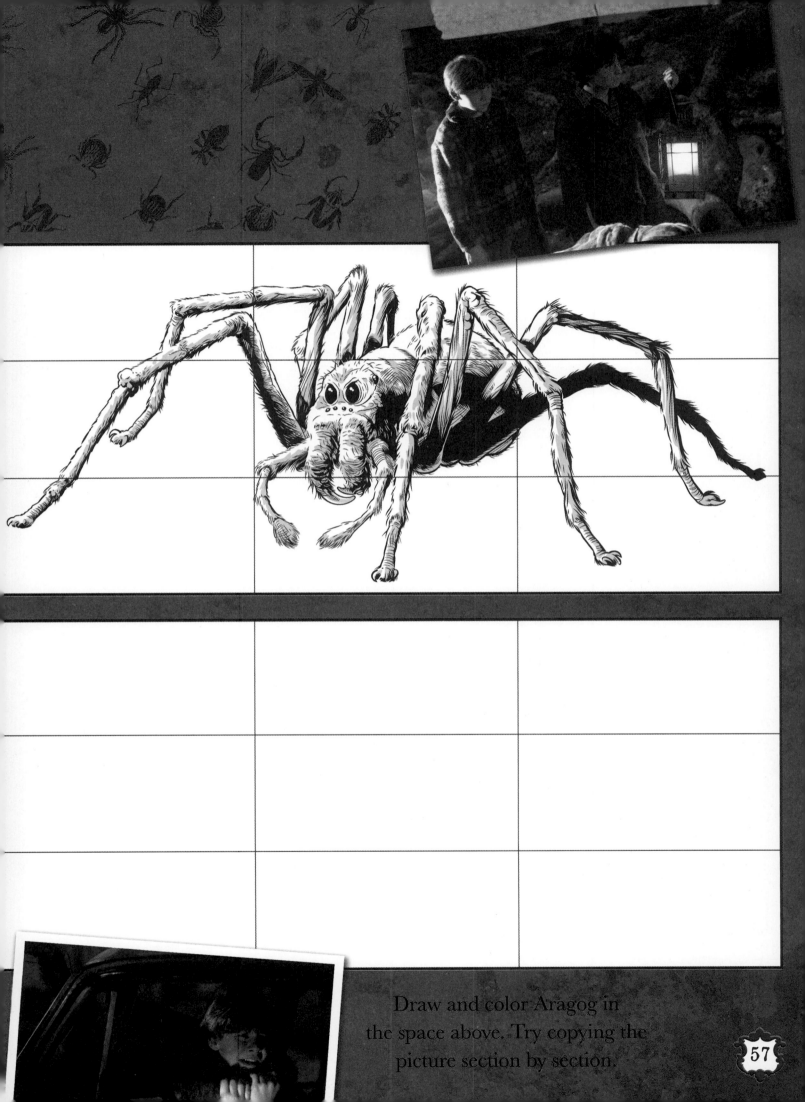

Draw and color Aragog in
the space above. Try copying the
picture section by section.

THE TRIWIZARD TOURNAMENT

The Triwizard Tournament is a magical contest held between three famous wizarding schools. Hogwarts, Durmstrang, and Beauxbatons compete to win the Triwizard Cup.

Viktor Krum

Fleur Delacour

Cedric Diggory

Harry Potter

Cedric Diggory puts his name into the Goblet of Fire to enter the Tournament.

The Triwizard Cup

The Triwizard Cup was at the center of the maze in the third and final task.

In the third task of the Triwizard Tournament, Harry has to battle his way through a magical maze.

Create your own maze on this page and challenge a friend to find their way through!

Magical Memories

Imagine that you've finished your first year at Hogwarts, and that you've grown into one of the finest young witches or wizards around.

Look back through this yearbook. What would your favorite moments from your first year be? Draw snapshots of them into the frames on these pages.

SLYTHERIN

RAVENCLAW

WEASLEY & WEASLEY